GRAVITY MAN

THE COMMENCEMENT

LUCIUS MAURICE (DAKSH)

My dedication is to Avengers for this book because I got the idea from themm of making a superhero series.Very very thanks to you . Next one is for The Superhero League . Because the names came from the same game . It is magnificient . I do recommend it to play . The next one is again for Notionpress who is accepting my every book submission . This is my third book . After this will come Steve and Alex Vs Death. I know you all will be enjoying it so yeah . Enjoy all of it . Because soon will come my app named Enjoy - The Masterpieces . So , stay tuned for more fiction .

Contents

Preface

It is written generally to make all of you enjoy . I started the superhero series to don't let go the magnificient fiction of this category . So , enjoy . Because this life has the base of only smile .

Prologue

Life did n't served anything good to Yusan whose life was worst because of family pressure , guilt and lies . But his life changes after gravitation rays are mixed with his blood and he becomes a superhero . He protects a building by not letting it fall he gets success in his first big mission . Now , he had a name - Gravity Man . But something other dangerous thing was waiting for him - Darker . Now , will he save the world or just see the world immersed in Darkness ruled by Darker .

CHAPTER ONE

My Common Life

I was just serving sushi to a customer when I saw Lin going past me . Her new gown caught my attention . It was white which was hiding her silky white legs . Let me tell you she always comes to know when I am staring her , she would turn and I would look the other side . I always missed her . Spending a second without seeing her was a year to me . It was just we had many chemistries in us . Means I cannot understand her and she cannot understand me . I always had a crush on her . Whenever I was cooking food or serving she would always look at me . I don't know if she was looking at the style of my cooking or at serving , but yeah she was looking .

CHAPTER TWO

A Offer is made

I was closing my little restaurant door upon which was hanging a noren when I saw her car parked right aside my shop . I was nervous . It was a black mercedes . The two bodyguards well mannered reached out to me and one of them said , " The madam want to talk to you ." I gone to her window and knocked . She opened it and said , " Hi , I am Lin , I have tasted your food , it is superb I want you to do the same at a party I am organizing, if you don't mind ." I said stammering , " Y-Y-Yes , Mam . " She said , " Good , my bodyguard will give you the address , date and time." Then she closed the window . It was a bit rough , but yeah , I still liked her . A bodyguard sat on a bike which belonged to her Bodyguarding council and then he was following her . Another one bodyguard said , " Come on or I will be late ." He said and offered me a seat beside his motorcycle . He asked , " I am Sheo . What is your name ? " I said, " Y-Y-Yusan . " He asked , " Why are you stammering ? " I took out a handkerchief , dried my face which was sweating and said, " I-I-I have T-Teptism - B . " I answered . He looked at me and asked , " What is it ? " I explained him it was disease in which you cannot socialize and it is difficult for you to meet and talk to strangers . He said , " I also had a friend Yusan . I called him Mr Best . " He continued , "

He and I were good friends . We studied in an NGO school located in Karuizawa . He was a very active and awesome looking but after sometime he became a blonde and lonely person . It carried on for four months remaining everyday absent . After that , on Friday 13th he done a school bunk and we never found him . It was said that he murdered a teacher and ran away . I begin to believe it a little because we saw a dead body of teacher Danna who was good to everybody except him because he was not good at Sugaku (Maths) . I miss him very much . He always had his father 's watch in his hand . A leathery gold colured watch . Oh , yeah , you have to come at 28th of this month at 8:00 p.m. to Barman club " I said , " That's my home . " He parked his motorbike right in front of a lane where my house was situated . We shooked hands and I was on my way to home . I did not looked back because I knew it would make me cry . I climbed the stairs, took my blanket and slept .

CHAPTER THREE

A Unusual dream which reveals a Secret

I woke up and saw I was in a home . A woman was cleaning shoes of some gentlemen in a nearby place with eyes on shoes and she was occasionaly looking sometimes at the bowl which had 27 yens in it that when the gentlemen will leave their fees . I had my face blank . Suddenly , a child ran to her . She said , " Hey my lovely chicken is back home ? How was your school ? " The child in his childish language said , " It is fantastic and the teachers are very good . " She smiled and taking her whole fees of the day 30 yens (3 yens were dropped by that gentlemen) , asked him " Will you go to your Hard working brother and ask him to give you food in these 5 yens ? " The child said , " Yeah , I would go he gives me gifts sometimes ." He said and ran towards a small restaurant . " Brother give me the food in these 5 yens . " came a order and a elderly person adjusted his glasses and said , " Oh , here it is my lovely chicken . Can I cook you ? " The child said , " No , don't cook me , cook food for me and my mother . " The elderly person bowed and said , " As you wish . " He then poured many noodles and putted them in 2 bowls . " Will you take it home ?" he asked . The child said , " Yeah , I am big now but in 5 yens there will only be one bowl why two ? " He took out a toffee out of his pocket and gave it to him saying , " These are my gifts to you." The child ran and told his mother the whole incident . But as his mother was listening him , she fainted . The 2 bowls and a toffee slipped from his hand , he shouted , " Help ! Help ! My mother has fainted ." The elderly person happened to pass by . He was taking a delivery and listening that words he throwed his bicycle there and ran to the direction . He took her in his arms and ran to the hospital nearby . I followed him . The Doctors done a immediate operation and said , " After this operation you have to give 2,000 yens to me. The elderly person and the child nodded and signed a form that they will give 2,000 yens to them . Now , they prayed and occasionally , she was saved . The child was the first to meet her . She said , " Hey , my little chicken see now I am fine . " The child still had tears in his eyes . He said , " What if you would have left me and became a fairy ? " The mother said , " I will always be with you . I will not become a fairy ." Suddenly, she cannot breathe the elderly person shouted , " Doctor , please help ." The doctors came running with a batch of nurses and the child and elderly person were asked to stay out I too gone with them out . The child asked , " Brother Naumbi , will mother be fine ? " Naumbi smiled , hugged him and said , "Yes , if you pray for her ." The child was praying . After 5 minutes , A doctor said , " She just have 15 minutes with her left . " Naumbi said , " My little chicken , go and meet her because after sometime she will become a fairy . " The child in horror ran to the room and said , " Mother , brother is saying that you will become a fairy , will you ? No , you will not leave me right ? " The mother said , " No , never , I will remain as a memory in your mind . When I will become a fairy , I will come in your dreams and if you would not have done your homework , I will say I am leaving . " But suddenly she said something from which child too understood that she became a fairy . She said , " Bye , my little chicken , Yusan . " I understood who she was and I shouted with the younger Yusan too with me . " No , you will not become a fairy . " Suddenly , I realized it was a day and the thing I saw was a nightmare .

CHAPTER FOUR

The Next tiring day

It was monday means today no restaurant opening going to the construction site as a labourer will be my today 's job . I had holidays on Sunday but yesterday I cannot find anything to do so I continued with the Restaurant . I woke up toasted some bread, while brushing my teeth , scrambled some eggs (I have to make it twice because the bubbles fall on the eggs of my toothpaste) , took a bath and wearing a construction site's labourer clothes gone to the nearby construction site . I lifted up almost 300 stones per day for which I would get 150 yens in my hand and 50 yens in my bank account . Today I lifted up 500 stone and got 250 yens in my hand and 50 yens in my bank account . Working on a day where the sun is boiling you , the weight of stones making you feel dizzy without even a single drink of water is not easy to work with . Finally , the day ended and I don't knew when i fall asleep on some stones there .

CHAPTER FIVE

I got some powers and my first mission too

" Hey ! Would you like to spend a night with me ? " said the first one . " No , let's take her to our apartment . " I reached there and asked , " Would you like to spend a night with me not in a apartment but here eating punches from me ?" The third one asked , " Who is this bastard ? " The second one said , " Let's make him realize who we are ? " The three were round him . I was thinking how to get out of this situation . I looked everywhere . There it was a bin . I concentrated and my left hand facing that bin .I opened my eyes . The orange magic was active . I took my hand backwards , it came close . With another hand holded it in the air and then my right hand controlling the bin was beating the three of them badly . I stretched my hands outwards and then they were saying , " Where is he ? " I was confused. I looked myself , I was invisible ! I then disabled my magic thinking let's fight with melee . I gave a punch to one and he was stunned . I now invisible , gone to them and my hand , I was just beating one of them with my hand on the head whenI saw something orange coming out of his head . He fainted . Seeing their friend not in senses they ran away from there .

CHAPTER SIX

I got the reason why the girl is here

I asked the girl how is she here ? She answered, " My parents are not supporting me in painting , so I ran away from there . " I asked , " Does your mother know about Leonardo Da Vinci ? " She answered , " My parents are crazy about him but they are not allowing me to do the same . " I offered , " I will talk with them . " She said , " No ,they will only be mad at me for leaving home , I want to pursue my carrer . " I said , " Just come with me . " I tried to form a platform which can move as I seen in Ben 10 but nope . She laughed . I said , " I was just trying . " We walked to the way home without uttering a single word . She finally said , " You are protecting me as if I am your sister . " I replied , " You are questioning me like I am your brother . " She laughed . We reached her home. She said going to the room to me , " Best of Luck ! "

CHAPTER SEVEN

I talked to her father

" I talked to her father , " Sir have you seen Monalisa painting ? " I asked . He said ,
" Yes " still in tension that her daughter will run away again . " You like Leonardo Da Vinci then why you don't like a Leonarda Da Vinci in your home ? Every father would like to see her daughter successive ? " He said , " She only have to learn how to handle housework . She is not capable of doing anything . By the way , I know her better that you , so keep your mouth shut and get lost . " A rage was growing inside me but still calm I said , " If she have to do just housework then why are you letting her paint . Inside yourself you know you want your daughter to be a Leonardo Da Vinci . " He now with anger and frustration said , " Who are you to interfere in my family matter ? " Now I cannot control my never ending anger . I burst out with rage , " Then see your daughter being run away once again . This time I happen to pass by or she would have been raped . But why would you worry ? You just cannot see beyond the end of your nose . Do you know what she said on her way home . I hate my father the most . I will get lost but see your daughter get lost in heaven . You freak . " I now gone on a bin's cover flying in sky home and slept .

CHAPTER EIGHT

A Murder

I woke up and found myself in a school . Sure enough that it is a nightmare . I saw that Teacher Danna going to his personal space . " Have you brought him ? " he asked someone . A man in white and green shirt and jeans nodded and gave him a pistol . The little Yusan was also seeing this . Danna asked the elderly person who was tied there with ropes , " Where are the 5,000 yens the monthly installment ? " Naumbi replied , " I have to buy food from them because Yusan had not eaten food since his mother died four months ago , so in hope that he would eat special food I took him to a restaurant . The whole money spent there . " Danna said , " His mother took loan from me @20% for her husband's operation . She would give me only a thousand yens a month . After she died , I thought her son would work for me and I would make the loan go down but you said you will pay the loan. It carried on till now and now you are saying that you don't have money ? " He throwed the pistol towards the door and said, " Now I will beat you this much your soul will too be frightened . " He said and kicked the Naumbi on the chest which forced some blood to come out and he was dead . He then lifted the elderly person up and throwed him out of the window . He drought a glass of water and said , " I have a plan . You all of you go out. " He said , " I will force a bullet in my hand and say that the elderly person because of a loan tried to kill me with his deep market bought pistol . Then , I would be saved . " He then was going towards the gun . Little Yusan lifted the pistol and forced a bullet in his heart . Then another one on his leg and screamed , " You killed my brother so now I will kill you . " He said and a bullet hitted the teacher's head . He ran . The police came after that and took both of them to hospital saying it is a murder and postmortem needd to be done . The reports came and it was told that Teacher Danna died because of a bullet and The elderly person died because of Commotio Cordis . The police said , " We will innquire about it . Maybe the elderly person killed the teacher then he killed himself jumping from the building . " I tried to say , No , teacher Danna killed him but

.

Sheo knows that I am his Mr Best

Suddenly , I woke up . I noticed today was 28th and I have to go to the Barman club . I dressed up in my best clothes because I knew today I have to go to the club after my restaurant . I opened the door and found the last night's girl on the door . But to my surprise there was already that person ready to pick me up . I said , " Hi Sheo , the party was at 8:00 p.m. I guess . He said , " Yup , but madam said that you have to be picked up and dressed in good clothes . By the way , you are not stammering now , is the disease gone ? " I sat on the back seat of his motorcycle and noticed that yeah I was not stammering after the power I got. I smiled and answered , " Yes . " He started hsi motorcycle and after five minutes I spotted the building . It paricularly had many people . Electricians were working on the fuses . The makeup artists were dressing some models . Sheo was saying hello to everyone on the way . He welcomed me in a room and gave me a dress on which was written - Chef of the Year . " I asked , " Sheo , why this ? " Sheo said , " It is because madam wants you to dress properly so that the guests in the party don't think that you are not a specialist . " He gave me a glare . I smiled but suddenly I saw a news on the television that a building was going down and fire brigade cannot hold it . I have to save it . I found my mask still with me . I said , " I will be back from the restroom . He nodded and I ran from the building . I was finding something on which I can go there . I found a bin cover there and yeah , I took it and flied on it . I reached there in an hour .The fire brigade was trying hard but of no use . I landed on a stump there. All were making my video there . I could hear the screams behind . I now with my orange magic tried to lift it up but in vain because my orange magic too cannot hold it . I done my full power . The nerves can be seen on my forehead and hands . I throwed it in the nearby big garbage heap . I then came down . I said , " It is okay . Nothing to worry about . " I was then just going when somebody asked , " Hey , what is your name , Superhero ?" I looked the ground first , thought and said , " Gravity Man . " I reached the building now , when I saw a hand over my shoulder . I looked back . It was a old fellow . He asked , " Can you tell me , where is the restroom ? " I pointed him a direction and said , " Over there . " He said , " I am blind . Can you leave me there ? " I said , " Yeah , why not . " I said that because I cannot find Sheo there . The news playing on the television caught my attention . " When there was no hope of any help , half a million lives were on stake , then a superhero named Gravity Man came and solved the problem . Now , there is very much craze in people . Some are making his tatoos , some are accusing him and some are regarding him as a miracle . " Suddenly , a feeble voice spoke out . " Can anyone tell me where is the restroom I am blind please help . I walked him to the restroom . When we reached there , I said , " Here it is . " The crampled voice came , " Thanks . Be careful . " The thanks was good enough to me . But that Be careful was like a bolt of lighting on me .

I was just cannot think about anything except that . What it meant ? I turned and found Sheo there . I don't know why but he was staring my hand . By the luck of fate , there was a golden leathery watch on my hand . It was revealed that his best friend Yusan was no more than me .

CHAPTER TEN

The Darker

He was still staring not able to believe that it was the very same watch . He did not said anything . After a while , he hugged me . The tear were coming out of his eyes . He said , " Where have you been Mr Best ? " I figured out that he was still a child who was crying for his best friend sorry , Mr Best . He after some while took me to the cafe and we drought a bottle of beer together . I said that , " Let's go to the club man . " He replied , " Let's go . " He cannot drink beer , because he did n't ever took the bad things like Cigrettes , etc . He cannot drive the bike anymore. So , I pursued him . I took him to the Barman club . By the time , we reached there it was 5:00 p.m. When I reached there a woman approached me and asked , " What would you need to make the dishes , sir ? " I ordered some fish , vegetables and rice with it . Those were my best dishes . I have to make all the food till 8:00 p.m. So , I started on . To my surprise , it was done till 7:30 p.m. All liked the food very much . I was just serving wine when I slipped and it fell on Lin's dress . I had my heart in the mouth . She screamed and kicked me out without even paying me . " Go to hell " came a voice behind me . I was crying that the hope of my love with her is too gone . But still I gone and slept .
I woke up and found myself in a dark room . It was not my

room . Suddenly , I saw many men coming to that room . Suddenly , I noticed that a person was standing aside me . He announced , " I want every drop of blood from Gravity Man's body . " All men were gone searching from me . Suddenly , another person emerged from the shadows . " Sir Darker , why this mission is being held ? Why only Gravity Man ? " Darkness said , " He has gravitation rays mixed in his blood which makes him Gravity Man . If I got that blood , I can be the ultimate Devil of this world . I will finish this world of feeble , innocent people . He will be killed .

CHAPTER ELEVEN

I am Revealed !

I found that it was morning . I turned on the radio want to hear some news . I want to ignore everything which Lin said me yesterday . " Bargo Construction Company is in trouble . The Founder and CEO's daughter is caught in a fire in a Barman club . It was reported that fire took place because of the burning of rags . Last time too , Gravity Man saved almost half a million lives . This time too people are looking forward to him . " I knew it was the time for action . I weared my mask and with my companion bin cover I reached there . I looked everywhere . There it was water . With my orange magic I took pile of water out and throwed it on the club . The fire was gone . I took everyone out . Lin was left . I picked her up in my arms . She struggled to pull my mask out . It was done . I have to leave her there . I snatched my mask , I then was flying on my bin cover to reach restaurant as soon as possible . I made my televison on . " The real face of Gravity Man is revealed . It is said that he is a restaurant owner . " ' My identity is revealed ' came into my mind . I decided to shut my restaurant as soon as possible . But as my came out , I saw a crowd of people running and coming towards me . I before even closing the restaurant ran with my bin cover . I locked myself in the room . Now , I even cannot go out . I tired gone on my bed

. I don't know when I got asleep .

I woke up and found myself in a dream . ' Here we go again . ' I thought . This time Darker was sleeping . Suddenly , the advisor bumped the door . The Darker woke up . " You stupid fool . Don't you know I was sleeping ? " The advisor came on his knees . " Sorry , Sir Darker but the news is such that you will jump on your feet if you came to know about it ? " He paused and then said , " The face of Gravity Man is revealed . " Darker's mouth was open . " If it is true then I will myself go to him . Now ! He then laughed loudly and said , " Get the armies ready . It is because Darker will now be the ultimate darkness of the world . "

CHAPTER TWELVE

I met Mr Ross

I woke up but this time I was sweating this much my shirt was wet and dark pouches can be seen there . I putted it in the washing machine and then it was being washed . I took a piece of bread and then I knew where I have to go . I took my companion bin with me and I flew over Washington then New York and reached Ross Industries .

I got on the counter , " Wanna meet Mr Ross . " The counterwoman said , " The name ? " I said , " Gravity Man ." She looked up and then called Mr Ross's telephone . " Sir Gravity Man on the counter . " There was a pause because I cannot hear anything . " Sir 3rd floor room no 7. " I have always preffered staircases so , yeah I gone there . I was going to knock when I came to know it was a automatic door . I entered . There it was Ronald Ross . He was not a very tall person . He had a average height . He did not had a beard . His hair were particularly in reddish shade .

" How are you Gravity Man ? " I said , " I am fine . Sir , I need some help from you . " He said , " Your name is Yusan . You are 25 years old . You were born in Karuizawa . You studied in a NGO School . You are a restaurant owner . You are in love with a famous businessmen's daughter Lin . But you have not talked to her yet . Your mother died because of a heart attack . Your brother died because of a loan and you also done a murder of your Maths teacher Danna . You live in street no.7 house no 36 pin code 429038 . " My mouth was open .

CHAPTER THIRTEEN

A New Shield and a Suit

" Close your mouth pal . " said the genius , intelligent outstanding memory holder Ronald Ross . He asked , " Why should I help you ? I know you would not have known my full name too . Ha ! Mother died , brother died , I don't know which sins you would have done in your previous birth ? " I cannot control anymore . I said , " Your full name is Ronald Edwin Ross . You were born in Chicago , USA . Your father was a scientist , inventor and a industrialist . He had 7 bank accounts with atleast 50 billion dollars in each . Then your father died because of by mistake drinking a drop of Hydrochloric Acid . Your mother was Japanese . So , you came here . Your mother married your stepfather who was a dealer in automobiles . You have a sister and a stepbrother . Your sister's name is Julie Edwin Ross . Your stepbrother's name is Evan John Williams . You started this company in 2001 . It became a marvel till 2003. You were thrown out of company 13 times . But thanks to your father's earnings you bought your company 12 times . At 13th time you done a fraud with help of your friend who is in the same company and you again have to be invited as CEO . Is this enough or you have to know something more ? " He said hiding his shock , " If you would have told my frauds too you would have been the head of Achievers . It is good that you only studied till 3rd class or you would have snatched my CEO seat . " I laughed . " Can we talk about buisness ? By the way , what is Achievers ? " he pressed a button and said, " I would help you defeating darker but on a condition , you have to wear the suits and shield I made for you and a vehicle too . You can have a favour from me anytime in the life . Here , you can choose any suit . He displayed a variety of suits . I was thrilled to see it . I began rating them . I got past a magnificient suit . Mr Ross seeing me said , " A very good suit . " I said , " Let's try this ." He clapped and some people came to take my measurements . They took it and said , " Lord Ross , it will be done within 5 minutes . " Mr Ross nodded . I asked , " Lord Ross ? " Mr Ross replied , " They call me . " Then , there was a pause . He continued , " I guess , now you don't have to wander in nightsuits . I laughed because I knew that he had seen nightsuit inside of my clothes . He then smiled at me . He then started to show me some shields . He showed me a red shield . " It will be a good one . " I thought , ' Nope . ' I saw a shield which had G engraved on it . " It is for me , I guess . " He said , " Nope , it's not for you . " I asked , " Why ? " He explained , " It was the first shield I made . I thought , ' Let's make a invincible shield . ' I experimented and it was made , but ? " I said , " But ? " He continued , " It got emotions in it . A unbreakable shield but it has very much power in it . I too cannot hold it . I done a research and found that it will choose its owner itself . I tried to use it but it done me a loss of 50,000 dollars . From that time , I had preserved it . It has lasers in it . I said , " Wow ! Let's hope it chooses me in the future . " I got past it and Mr Ross recommended me a simple shield which I chose because it had same power as me .

CHAPTER FOURTEEN

Darker's Defect is found

I asked , " Can we find Darker's location ? " I was just completing my sentence when he said , " Found in Tokyo . He is harming people near Tokyo tower ." Mr Ross said . Try my vehicle . He said and handed me over the shield . I with help of my orange magic controlled my shield and gone flying over Tokyo tower . There it was Darker . He wore a black blanket which was hiding his face . I landed with my shield in the hand . " I knew that you will come here " he said . " Let me introduce me to you . My name is..." He was just saying when I said , " Your name is Darker . Your motive is to be the ultimate darkness of the world . You also send your useless troops but they too cannot find me . When you heard my face is revealed you jumped up and down . To be the ultimate Darkness of the world , you need my blood in which gravitation rays are mixed . By the way , where is your useless amature advisor ? " He said , " Have done your homework . " Then he laughed . I took some stones out of the Earth and thowed them to his side . He disappeared and appeared just beside me . I tried to do something with amy orange magic but of no use . I remembered a law of science . ' When there is a gravitational circle around a person who can teleport he cannot teleport anymore .' I formed a circle around him . Then I formed a circle around him so that he cannot teleport . He bumped into a shop with light in it . I saw as the light fall on him his skin burned . He made it hide with his cloak . I made myself hide beside a shop and called Mr Ross. " Mr Ross when Darker is being exposed to light his skin burns , is there any way to kill him by this method . " Mr Ross said after a while , ' I think when he is being exposed to light , his skin which is dark cannot hold it anymore . Get him exposed to light .' I thought to get the largest light source in the city , yeah , a watchtower .

CHAPTER FIFTEEN

I am kidnapped

I got my shield and was just flying when Darker attacked me , I throwed a bulb at him the tungsten in it burned his skin so much that his veins were visible . " You bastard . " I have to run I reached the watchtower in about 15 minutes . I flashed the light on him but of no use . The tungston was very little in it . I now understood light was not his weakness the tungsten was his weakness . I was just gonna call Mr Ross when I thought someone hitted me on the head from the back . I fainted . I opened my eyes and I found myself naked with only underwear on a patient bed . I tried to get up but my hands and feet were tied . Suddenly , I saw a iphone on the bed nearby . I remembered that by saying Hey Siri I can call anyone and Mr Ross too have a iphone . I remembered Mr Ross's phone number and said the words . I knew that if the setting was turned on a specific voice it would be of no use but if setting is on everyone , it will be a major profit . " Hey Siri ! Call 1773 862 5789 .

CHAPTER SIXTEEN

I am freed but Darker

My fate came into serving . It was calling . " Yusan ! " Mr Ross said that as if he knew that it was me . I said , " Mr Ross please free me up . Trace this phone's location , hack this system and get me out of this heck . " " I will get you out . " He said and I was freed. I took the phone and said , " How ? " He said , " Hey ! I am the founder of Ross Industries , I can do it quickly ." I saw a gentlemen's dress hanging on there . I wore it and checked the whole room . I found a knife and a file over there . I read it and found 3.5 litres of my blood was taken out . I peeped out of the window and found it was a military train . It was taking Armour piercing Fragiles made purely of tungsten . I got the idea and took a flashlight with me which was lying in a dustbin over there . I grabbed on my shield and found the Darker in the next compartment. I saw he became powerful . I found that fragiles were in that room too . I found a idea . I entered the room , got a fragile and ran to the junkyard .

CHAPTER SEVENTEEN

Mr Ross got a Missile Launcher

I called Mr Ross and said , " I want a missile launcher now . " Mr Ross rushed to the Military base and said , " Want a missile launcher . " A solider replied , " And you think we will give it ? " Mr Ross said , " You will give it if you get a consent from prime minister ? " The solider replied , " Of course ! " Mr Ross got the prime minister's phone number by hacking . He said , " Prime Minister Natumbo Maisaka talking ? " Came the answer , " Yeah ! Who is this ? " Mr Ross explained him the whole issue . The prime minister said , " Okay , you can take it . " He said and the base got a order right then . Mr Ross was handed over the missile launcher . He reached his laboratory . He with help of his drone servicer sent that launcher to him right then . The Darker was also searching the junkyard for Yusan . Yusan was sitting beside a heap of garbage and found a great black shadow over him . I took a heap of garbage , with help of my orange magic and throwed it straight to Darker's face . I ran and found that missile launcher had came . I was just loading the fragile in it . When Darker came beside me . As he reached me , I done my shield before him and he bumped directly into it . I loaded fragile successfully in the missile launcher . But Darker I was just shooting him when he punched me down.

Darker is dead

He picked me up with one arm and was just gonna punch me with the other when I said , " Face your death because it is just beside you . " Darker said , " You are lying . " I said , " Bye ! You are also gonna die with me ." He cannot control and looked beside him there was nothing . He was turned round and found that I was using my orange magic . He said , " Now you will die . " I said , " Happy death because now you will die . " I disabled my orange magic and the loaded missile launcher fell to ground . The missile came out and it directly hitted Darker . He laughed and said , " What a missile will do to me ? " I said , " Yeah , a missile will do nothing to you unless it is made of tungsten . " He has his eyes big . Suddenly , there was a explosion . It left me unconscious . My eyes were being closed when I saw Doctor Ross coming towards me . My eyes were closed .

CHAPTER NINETEEN

Lin came to see me

Next, I woke up in my house . There was a package and note on the nearby table . It read - Hey chap ! Are you fine ? You know that it was a marvellous adventure . I with help of prime minister released a statement that the rumours are false . All is well . Your shield was broken so in this package are some gifts from me . I have to see another champ in my laboratory so I have to go . Don't mind , open it , be happy and call me .' I opened the package and found some fabulous things inside . There was the G Engraved Shield , one more shield and a orange suit . It had another note with it . It read - This suit and fantastic shield from me , I know that you will not use the special shield , that's why I sent another one . Because of this suit because now you don't have to go here and there for saving people in the nightsuits .' I remembered that line which he said on my first visit to him . Today was Sunday so I wore my suit , wore my mask and took another one shield with me instead of that special one and I opened my door to go and I saw Lin over there . Her eyes were looking up and then she said , " I love you . Marry me . " I smiled with a wide grin on my face remembering my past and said , " GO-TO-HELL . " I slammed the door and determined to leave from my garden by flying . I could hear her saying , " If he would have married me it could be a great publicity . Now I have to marry that famous filmstar . "

CHAPTER TWENTY

A new normal for me

I decided to leave after having a coffee . I sat with a chair in the sun drinking the coffee . I was now thinking about my personal life . ' Who will be my wife ? Whom can I trust ? ' I was looking at sky when thinking all this . I saw something flying going over the sky . My binoculars were on my lap so I saw it . It was another maleficent superheroine . I cannot see her face except a cheap ruby ring on her hand . I knew from that instance that she was what I was looking for answers . I knew that she was my wife . I wanna go after her but I now can hear screams in the neighbourhood about theft so gonna go that way . But we will meet again . It's my promise . I thought to myself . Then I gone gliding in the sky towards another destination . Because it was now a new normal to me .